A Beginning-to-Read Book

Dear Dragon Gets a Hole-in-One

by Margaret Hillert

Illustrated by Jack Pullan

NORWOOD HOUSE PRESS

DEAR CAREGIVER,

The *Beginning-to-Read* series is a carefully written collection of classic readers you may remember from your own childhood. Each book features text comprised of common sight words to provide your child ample practice reading the words that appear most frequently in written text. The many additional details in the pictures enhance the story and offer the opportunity for you to help your child expand oral language and develop comprehension.

Begin by reading the story to your child, followed by letting him or her read familiar words and soon your child will be able to read the story independently. At each step of the way, be sure to praise your reader's efforts to build his or her confidence as an independent reader. Discuss the pictures and encourage your child to make connections between the story and his or her own life. At the end of the story, you will find reading activities and a word list that will help your child practice and strengthen beginning reading skills.

Above all, the most important part of the reading experience is to have fun and enjoy it!

Shannon Cannon

Shannon Cannon, Ph.D.
Literacy Consultant

Norwood House Press • P.O. Box 316598 • Chicago, Illinois 60631
For more information about Norwood House Press please visit our website at *www.norwoodhousepress.com* or call 866-565-2900.

Text copyright ©2016 by Margaret Hillert. Illustrations and cover design copyright ©2016 by Norwood House Press, Inc. All rights reserved. No part of this book may be reproduced or utilized in any form or by any means without written permission from the publisher.

LIBRARY OF CONGRESS CATALOGING-IN-PUBLICATION DATA
    Hillert, Margaret.
      Dear Dragon gets a hole-in-one / by Margaret Hillert ; illustrated by Jack Pullan.
        pages cm. -- (A Beginning-to-read book)
      Summary: "A boy and his pet dragon go mini-golfing for the first time.
    With help from Father, they learn how to play golf, and even get a
    hole-in-one! This title includes reading activities and a word list"-- Provided by publisher.
      ISBN 978-1-59953-705-4 (library edition : alk. paper) -- ISBN
    978-1-60357-795-3 (ebook)
    [1. Miniature golf--Fiction. 2. Golf--Fiction. 3. Dragons--Fiction.] I.
    Pullan, Jack, illustrator. II. Title.
      PZ7.H558Ddr 2015
      [E]--dc23
                              2014043661

275N—062015
Manufactured in the United States of America in Stevens Point, Wisconsin.

Come on!
Come on!

Sir Putts-a-Lot
GOLF KINGDOM

3

What is this spot?
What can we do here?

4

You will see.
You will need this and this.

You have to get the ball in that hole.

Oh that is not good.
I will do it one more time.

9

Father, can you do it?
Can you do it?

Father, you are so good!
The ball is in the hole.

Oh, what a funny worm.
It is in a hole too.
I will make it get out.

That did not work!
The ball is not in.

I put the ball in!
Oh boy!

Look at this big house.
Let's try this one.
One ball for you —
And one ball for me.

We did it!
There are two balls in the hole now.

Look at this one.
It is down here.
But it will go up, up, up in the sky.

No, no.
It cannot go up.

But you can put your ball in the hole.

Come this way.
Look what I see here.

It looks like you, Dear Dragon!

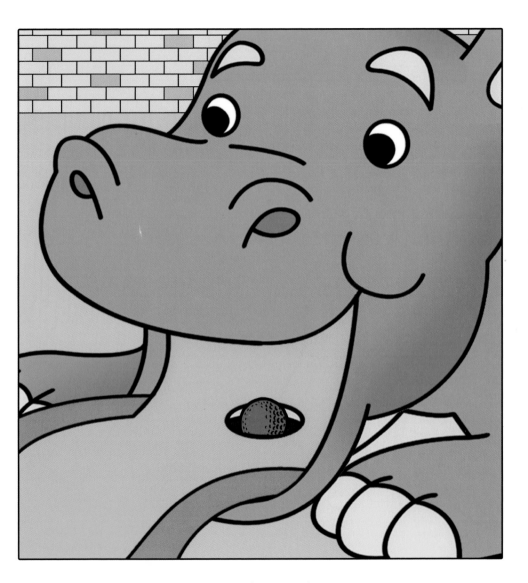

HOLE-IN-ONE!!!

Here you are with me.
And here I am with you.
Oh what a fun day, Dear Dragon.

29

The following activities support the findings of the National Reading Panel that determined the most effective components for reading instruction are: Phonemic Awareness, Phonics, Vocabulary, Fluency, and Text Comprehension.

Phonemic Awareness: Syllabication

Say the following words, clapping the syllables as you say them. Ask your child to tell you how many syllables are in each word:

happy–2	hole–1	Father–2	funny–2
pretty–2	ball–1	cannot–2	dragon–2
one–1	club–1	something–2	hit–1

Phonics: The letter Hh

1. Demonstrate how to form the letters **H** and **h** for your child.

2. Have your child practice writing **H** and **h** at least 3 times each.

3. Ask your child to point to the words in the book that start with the letter **h**.

4. Write down the following words and ask your child to circle the letter **h** in each word:

happy	help	hit	hand
father	this	here	hole
where	how	the	help

Vocabulary: Naming Objects

1. Ask your child to tell you different words he or she thinks of that go with mini-golf. Write the words on sticky notes and have the child place them next to any objects he or she has named that are in the story.

2. Ask your child to tell a story using all of the words he or she has come up with that relate to mini-golf.

Fluency: Choral Reading

1. Reread the story to your child at least two more times while your child tracks the print by running a finger under the words as they are read. Ask your child to read the words he or she knows with you.

2. Reread the story aloud together. Be careful to read at a rate that your child can keep up with.

3. Repeat choral reading and allow your child to be the lead reader and ask him or her to change from a whisper to a loud voice while you follow along and change your voice.

Text Comprehension: Discussion Time

1. Ask your child to retell the sequence of events in the story.

2. To check comprehension, ask your child the following questions:

   • What game/sport can you play at Golf Kingdom?

   • What are some things you need in order to play golf?

   • If you have played mini-golf, did you have a favorite hole? If not, what was your favorite hole in this story?

WORD LIST

Dear Dragon Gets a Hole-in-One **uses the 71 words listed below.**

The **5** words bolded below serve as an introduction to new vocabulary, while the other 66 are pre-primer. You may wish to write the words on index cards and use them to help your child build automatic word recognition. Regular practice with these words will enhance your child's fluency in reading connected text.

a	father	let's	put	way
am	for	like		we
and	fun	look(s)	see	what
are	funny		**sky**	will
at		make	so	with
	get	me	spot	work
ball(s)	go	more		**worm**
big	good		that	
boy		need	the	you
but	have	no	there	your
	here	not	this	
can	hole	now	**time**	
cannot	**house**		to	
come		oh	too	
	I	on	try	
day	in	one	**two**	
dear	is	out		
did	it		up	
do				
down				
dragon				

ABOUT THE AUTHOR Margaret Hillert has written over 80 books for children who are just learning to read. Her books have been translated into many different languages and over a million children throughout the world have read her books. She first started writing poetry as a child and has continued to write for children and adults throughout her life. A first grade teacher for 34 years, Margaret is now retired from teaching and lives in Michigan where she likes to write, take walks in the morning, and care for her three cats.

Photograph by Glenna Washburn

ABOUT THE ILLUSTRATOR A talented and creative illustrator, Jack Pullan, is a graduate of William Jewell College. He has also studied informally at Oxford University and the Kansas City Art Institute. He was mentored by the renowned watercolor artists, Jim Hamil and Bill Amend. Jack's work has graced the pages of many enjoyable children's books, various educational materials, cartoon strips, as well as many greeting cards. Jack currently resides in Kansas.